KU-595-427

INSECTOIDS

ROGER HURN

Insectoids ISBN 978-1-78147-965-0

Text © Roger Hurn 2014
Complete work © Badger Publishing Limited 2014

All rights reserved. No part of this publication may be
reproduced, stored in any form or by any means mechanical,
electronic, recording or otherwise without the prior permission
of the publisher.

The right of Roger Hurn to be identified as author of this Work has
been asserted by him in accordance with the Copyright, Designs and
Patents Act 1988.

Publisher: Susan Ross
Senior Editor: Danny Pearson
Publishing Assistant: Claire Morgan
Copyeditor: Cheryl Lanyon
Designer: Bigtop Design Ltd

2 4 6 8 10 9 7 5 3 1

CHAPTER 1

BAD NEWS

Matthew and Gemma stared at the class of sulky eleven-year-olds. Matt and Gem weren't teachers. They were battle-hardened Shadow Rangers, but they were only a few years older than the kids they faced. They glanced at each other. They were both thinking the same thing.

"I'd rather be in a fire fight with a swarm of mutant Insectoids than here," Matt muttered.

"Me too," whispered Gemma. "But orders are orders."

The kids' teacher cleared her throat. "Now class," she said. "We have two Shadow Rangers with us today." She smiled at Matt and Gemma. The class didn't. "They're going to explain to you why studying hard in school is the best way you can help Rangers like them win the war against the Insectoids."

The class did not look impressed.

Matt stepped forward and opened his mouth to speak, but the class had other ideas.

"Why do we have to learn boring stuff in school?" demanded a boy with a freckled face and spiky hair. "You're Shadow Rangers. You should be teaching us how to fight the bugs!"

Before either Matt or Gemma could reply, a girl at the back of the class shouted out, "Yeah, 'cos what are we going to do when the Insectoids attack… read them a story?"

Matt held up his hand for silence. The class glared at him. "Look, you'll get your chance to fight the bugs when you're older… and we'll train you up to do just that when the time comes, OK? But that's not what today is all about."

The class still glared at him. "So what is today all about then?" said the girl at the back.

"It's about teaching you guys how to use your brains," said Gemma. "The Insectoids aren't mindless bugs… they're clever. So we don't need cannon fodder if we're going to beat them… we need bright people who can outsmart them."

"Gemma's right, guys. So listen up and you may just learn something that'll save your life when the time comes."

Before any of the children could reply, the door opened and a tall, tough-looking man strode in. Matt and Gemma snapped to attention and saluted. It was General Carter, the Shadow Rangers' Commander. He had a grim expression on his face. "Class dismissed," he said. The children grabbed their books and hurried out with their teacher.

When they'd gone, General Carter turned to Matt. "I've bad news, Ranger. Your parents and sister have been captured in a raid by an Insectoid snatch squad."

"What!" Matt was stunned.

"The Insectoids killed everyone else, but made off with your family. It seems that they were the target. We have no idea why."

Gemma shook her head. "Who can second-guess bugs?"

"It doesn't matter why they've taken my family," snarled Matt. "All that matters is rescuing them. So I'm out of here. I can follow the Insectoids' trail into the badlands and hunt them down."

General Carter shook his head. "I'm afraid I can't allow you to do that."

Matt did a double-take. "You're kidding me, right?"

General Carter glared at him. He didn't like it when anyone questioned his authority.

"Look, I'm sorry about your parents, Ranger, but I have to see the bigger picture. I can't let you go running off looking for revenge. That's not how it works. You have a job to do here, so that's what you'll do until I decide otherwise – and that's an order!"

Matt shook his head. "No, *I'm* sorry, General," he said, "that's one order you can stick where the sun don't shine!"

Then, before either the General or Gemma could stop him, Matt stormed off.

"He didn't mean that, General," said Gemma. "He's just really upset about his family being kidnapped." Then Gemma ran out after Matt.

The General didn't move. He clenched his fists and a furious light burned in his eyes. "Even if he makes it back alive he's finished as a Ranger in my command," he muttered to himself. "Nobody, but nobody, speaks to me like that. I'll make him wish he'd never been born!"

CHAPTER 2

BADLANDS

Matt was a skilled tracker and, after a couple of hours of following the Insectoids' trail, he came out of a dense wood and spotted the snatch squad about half a mile ahead of him. The Insectoids were taking his family across a field that was choked with weeds. The going was hard but the bugs nipped Matt's family with their sharp claws every time they showed signs of slowing down.

Suddenly, Matt's younger sister Kerry tripped and fell. She was exhausted. For a second, Matt thought the Insectoids were going to kill her.

They jabbed at her and drool dripped from their jaws. Kerry began to scream.

"No!" yelled Matt, but he was too far away to help. Then the largest of the bugs screeched and the Insectoids backed off. Kerry scrambled up and ran to her parents. Her mum hugged her and Matt's dad shouted at the bugs. The creatures ignored him. He was no threat to them.

The bugs moved away from his family and chittered to each other. Matt had no idea what they were saying. It didn't matter. It was the opportunity he had been waiting for.

Matt's family were sitting by an overgrown hedge at the edge of the field. He crawled through the long grass until he reached it. Then he jumped up and blasted the Insectoids with deadly foam from his blaster.

The Insectoids were taken completely by surprise. Matt charged at them, covering them with foam. Their hard skins melted and they dissolved before Matt's eyes.

"Matt, look out!" his sister yelled a warning, but it was too late! A huge winged bug swooped down from the sky and crashed into him. Matt was knocked out cold.

When Matt came round he couldn't move. The Insectoid had wrapped him up in a sticky cocoon. Only Matt's head was free. The hideous creature scuttled over to him. Its long jaws clacked together like two sharp knives. Matt was sure it was about to bite his head off.

The terrifying bug loomed over him. Matt could see his own face reflected over and over again in its eyes. Then the creature's mouth opened and a harsh sound grated on Matt's ears. It was speaking!

"You failed in your mission, Shadow Ranger. Now you will die."

Matt wasn't going to beg for his life, but he wanted to know if his family had escaped. "Just tell me, did I free my family?"

A horrid screeching filled the air. Matt realised that it was the Insectoid laughing.

"No, you didn't. We have taken them to a holding pen next to our Hive. We will feed them to our Queen. They will be eaten alive, Shadow Ranger." The creature screeched its horrible laugh again.

Even though he knew it was hopeless, Matt wasn't about to give up. "OK, bug, do your worst. But, this isn't the end. When I'm dead other Rangers will finish what I've started. They'll come and destroy your Queen and her Hive."

The bug shook its head. "They can try but the Hive is in the glass tower that you humans call the Shard. It is a fitting place for our Queen to live." The Insectoid thrust its ugly head close to Matt. Matt could feel its foul breath on his face. It stank of death. "The Shard is too high and well protected for your Rangers to approach it without being seen. We will crush them."

"Yeah, you wish, bug. Here's one Ranger you didn't see coming!"

The Insectoid spun round. Gemma was standing there with her blaster locked and loaded. She squeezed the trigger and the full force of a jet of insecticide foam hit the bug right between the eyes. It never stood a chance.

"Gemma!" gasped Matt. "What the hell are you doing here?"

"Saving your backside," replied Gemma as she used a pocket laser to cut away the sticky threads of the Insectoid cocoon and free Matt.

Matt leaped back up onto his feet. He grinned at his friend and they tapped fists.

"Did General Carter change his mind and send you after me?" he asked.

"No way! He's furious with you and ordered me to stay put."

"What! You disobeyed a direct order?" Matt was shocked. Gemma was the kind of person who always did things by the book. He realised that she must like him an awful lot to do what she'd done. *That's good,* he thought, *because I'd have done the same for her. Though no way am I admitting it!*

"Yes," said Gemma. "And it's lucky for you I did because, if I hadn't, you'd be dead meat."

Matt nodded. "You're right, Gem. I owe you big time." Then he frowned. "Look, I'm in trouble with General Carter, but if you go back to Shadow Ranger HQ right now, you'll be OK. He won't even know you've been gone."

Gemma folded her arms and glared at him. "Do you really think I'm going to leave you out here to face the bugs on your own?" She shook her head. "Dream on, buddy, that so isn't going to happen. We're a team, Matt. Don't even think about trying to go it alone!"

Matt gave her the ghost of a smile. "OK, Gem, but rescuing my family is going to be a tough ask."

Gemma looked thoughtful. "Maybe… but I heard that bug tell you where they were taking your folks, and why… so what are we waiting for?"

CHAPTER 3

THE UNDERGROUNDERS

The once-great cities of the world were now a mess of broken buildings and rubble-strewn roads… and London was no exception. There was a reason for this. Many years earlier, a mutant species of insects had evolved deep underground. The Insectoids were clever but cruel and they wanted to rule the earth. However, they knew they had to wait until the time was right.

Then, when the Ebola virus swept across the globe killing countless millions, the Insectoids saw that their day had come. They poured out of their lairs and launched their attack.

Humanity tried to fight back but, already
devastated by the virus, they didn't stand
a chance. The ruthless mutants destroyed
everything and everyone who stood in their way.

Then, when the war was done, the Insectoids
took over the cities and towns. The few remaining
humans fled and hid wherever they could find
shelter from the wrath of the Insectoids.

However, when the survivors grew tired of
living like animals, a band of warriors called
the Shadow Rangers led the fight back. Now
Matt and Gemma were taking the fight into
the heart of London. It was madness… but
they had no choice.

Matt and Gemma slipped along the shattered
streets. Then Matt held up his hand. "Listen up,
Gem, I can hear Insectoids coming."

The two Rangers ducked behind the
tumbledown wall of a ruined house. They were
not a moment too soon. As soon as they'd taken

cover, a swarm of gruesome Insectoids came scuttling round the corner of the street. They were herding a captured group of terrified humans.

"Come on, Gem," whispered Matt. "No way am I going to let those bugs feed any more of our guys to their Queen."

He started to rise, but Gemma pulled him back behind the wall.

"No," she said. "There are too many Insectoids for us to take out here. Let's tag along behind them and wait for a better opportunity to strike."

"OK," said Matt, "we'll follow them… but make sure they don't see you."

"Wow! Thanks for the advice," said Gemma. "I would never have thought of that all by myself! Duh!"

Matt didn't reply. It seemed to him that fighting bugs was way easier than trying to understand girls. He just primed his blaster and made to set off after the Insectoids. Gemma did the same, but they were both halted in their tracks when a voice said, "I wouldn't do that if I were you."

They spun round, blasters at the ready, and came face to face with a scruffy-looking boy of about fifteen. The boy held up his hands. "Hey, take it easy guys, I'm not an Insectoid. I'm Ryan and I'm an Undergrounder."

"What the hell is an Undergrounder?" snapped Matt.

The boy shrugged. "We're people who live in the tunnels of the London Underground. We only come up to the surface to find food." He pulled a face. "It's not great down there, but the mutants tend to leave us alone. I guess it's their idea of a sick joke that humans, not bugs, have to live in holes in the ground now."

Gemma nodded. "But at least you're alive."

Ryan shook his head sadly. "If you can call hiding in tunnels living," he replied.

Matt frowned, "So, what are you doing up here on the surface?"

"Saving your lives!" exclaimed Ryan. "Listen, if you'd gone after those bugs, you'd have walked smack into an Insectoid patrol of mutant scorpions." The boy was jumpy and scared even though he was trying hard not to show it. "Look, I know you're a couple of hot-shot Shadow Rangers but, trust me, those things would've wasted you big time."

Matt narrowed his eyes. "Maybe," he said, "but we can take care of ourselves."

"Sure you can," said the boy. "But if you want to rescue those people, there's a better way to do it than picking a fight you can't win."

Matt raised his eyebrows. "Really? What's that?"

"The bugs take captured humans to a sports'

stadium near the Shard. They keep them there until they're ready to eat them." He shuddered. "But I know how we can get there without the bugs seeing us."

"OK," said Matt. "How?"

Ryan grinned. "Easy," he said. "We'll take the Underground route."

CHAPTER 4

A PLAN

Ryan took the two Shadow Rangers through a maze of rubble-filled back alleys to an old Underground station. He pulled a torch out of his pocket. It didn't give off much light, but it was just enough to show a set of steps going down into the darkness.

"Sorry, the lifts don't work," he said. "Still, going up and down all these steps keeps you fit. So, let's go. Just try not to trip up, OK?"

At the foot of the stairs was a platform. Ryan walked to its edge and jumped down onto the tracks. Matt and Gemma stared at him. "It's safe," he said. "There's no power and no trains coming." He turned and walked off into the tunnel. The Shadow Rangers took a deep breath and followed him.

It was a grim place. The air was filled with dust that scratched their eyes and made them choke. Rats ran over their feet, their red eyes reflected in the torchlight.

"How can you live in a place like this?" Gemma asked.

"I don't live… I survive," said Ryan. "The two things aren't the same." He sounded bitter and angry. "Plus, I don't have a choice."

"You will when we defeat the Insectoids," said Matt.

"Yeah? Well, let's crack on then," replied Ryan. "Because that day can't come soon enough for me."

The little group stumbled on until they came to another station. "Here we are," said Ryan. He climbed up onto the platform. He handed the torch to Matt. "This is as far as I go. You guys are on your own now."

"Hey, won't you need the torch to find your way back?" asked Gemma.

Ryan shook his head. "Don't worry about me. I've spent so long living down here I've almost learned how to see in the dark." He gave them the thumbs-up. "Good luck, guys… you're gonna need it." Then he hopped back down onto the track and stumbled off into the darkness.

Matt turned to Gemma. "Right, it's time to hit that stadium!"

Gemma didn't move.

Matt frowned. "Hey, Gem, what's up? You're not getting cold feet are you?"

She shook her head. "No, but I am getting a good idea."

Matt was unconvinced. "Yeah? What is it?"

Gemma pulled out a hand-held computer from her pocket. She tapped the screen and then smiled. "Look, Matt, when they built the Shard back in the old days they also built a secret Underground line to the main railway track."

He was puzzled. "Why would they do that?"

"Because a lot of very rich guys had offices in the Shard. They wanted to be able to come and go without mixing with regular people. But the point is, we can use that tunnel to get right underneath the Shard."

"How does that help?"

"It helps because we can then sneak into the Shard's basement."

Matt was still puzzled. "Why would we do that?"

"Because the gas supply meter that powers the whole building is there. All we have to do is put explosive charges on it. We set the timer to go off after we've gone. Then, when it blows up, it'll take out the Hive and the Queen with one big bang. Simple!"

Matt rubbed his chin. "Great, but what about the bugs guarding the stadium? How do we get rid of them?"

"We don't."

Matt stared at Gemma. "What do you mean? We have to get rid of them!"

Gemma smiled. "No, they'll get rid of themselves. The big bang will freak the bugs out. They'll panic and rush off back to the Hive to see what's happened."

Matt grinned at Gemma. "Gem, did I ever tell you you're a genius?"

"No," she said. "But you can tell me I'm a genius after the plan's worked!"

CHAPTER 5

THE BASEMENT

The secret station was as quiet as the grave. Matt and Gemma crept along the platform to the exit. They left a trail of footprints in the thick dust.

"This isn't good," said Gemma. "If any bugs come along, they'll see our trail."

"True," said Matt, "but there are no bug tracks in the dirt so I don't think they know about this place."

"I hope you're right. It's already creepy enough down here. The last thing we need is mutant Insectoids for company." Gemma shivered even though it wasn't cold.

There was a lift up to the Shard. It looked as if it hadn't been used in years.

"Where's the basement?" whispered Matt.

Gemma checked the map on her tablet. "It's down a set of steps near the lift," she said.

Matt shone his torch beam into the shadows. He saw the steps. Something scuttled away down them.

"What was that?" Gemma sounded really jumpy.

Matt gulped. "I think it was a rat. A big rat, maybe… but just a rat."

At the bottom of the steps they came to a door. It was locked.

"Well, what did you expect, Matt?" said Gemma. "A welcome mat?"

She took out her laser and aimed a jet of red-hot laser light at the lock. The metal sizzled and melted. When she was done, Matt raised his foot and kicked the door open. He had his blaster at the ready, but the room was empty.

Gemma peered into the gloom. Then she smiled with relief. "There's the meter on the wall. Let's fix the charges and get the hell out of here."

"How long shall I set the timer for?"

Gemma shrugged. "I guess sixty minutes will give us plenty of time to make it back to the stadium."

"OK, then," said Matt. "Sixty minutes it is." He punched in the time and the red digital clock began its countdown. Then, just as he and Gemma were about to leave, they heard a chittering noise from outside the basement.

CHAPTER 6

TRAPPED!

Matt's mouth went dry and Gemma's heart missed a beat. There was at least one Insectoid outside the room.

"We need to lead them away from here," whispered Matt. "If they find the charge our big plan is toast."

Gemma didn't answer. She was studying the map on her tablet. Then she looked up and spoke. "Here's what we do, Matt." She pointed to a metal grille on the wall. "We unscrew that grille and drop it on the floor. The bugs will hear the noise and dash in here. They'll think we've

sneaked into the Shard via the ventilation shaft.
They'll go in there after us and won't stop to
search the basement for us, or the bomb…
I hope!"

Matt didn't waste any time. He pulled the grille
off the wall. Gemma ducked behind a pile of
boxes. Matt let the metal grille fall with a loud
clang. Then he dived across the room and nearly
knocked Gemma over as he piled into her hiding
place. She glared at him, but before she could say
anything, a bug burst through the door. A spooky,
green glow came from its body.

The Insectoid scuttled over to the shaft opening.
It reared up and peered inside. Then it dropped
back down and rubbed its back legs together.
It was an alarm call and the shrill sound was as
sharp and painful as a knife.

Matt and Gemma slapped their hands over their
ears to try and block it out. The row seemed to
last forever. Then, just when they thought their
heads would split open, the noise stopped. This

wasn't good news. The bug had no need to keep the alarm going. It had been joined by more bugs.

Matt risked a quick look at them. The sight made his blood turn to ice. The new bugs were two-tailed mutant scorpions.

The scorpions screeched at the glow bug. Matt didn't need to speak Insectoid to know they were angry.

Matt held his breath. He needed the bugs to go off on a wild-goose chase. Then one of them scrambled up into the shaft. It was a tight squeeze, but it made it. One by one the others followed until there was only the first bug left in the room. Matt allowed himself to breathe again.

Gemma jabbed Matt in the ribs. She pointed to the timer on her tablet. The bomb was due to go off in forty minutes. Time was fast running out. The problem was, the bug showed no sign of moving. Matt guessed the scorpions had told it to stay and guard the shaft.

Another ten minutes ticked by. Still the bug stayed put. Now there were only thirty minutes left until the blast. Matt and Gemma knew they had to do something. But they couldn't risk attacking the creature because it would raise the alarm. They couldn't sneak past it either as it stood between them and the door. They were trapped.

Five more minutes slipped away. Things were now really desperate. The Shard was twenty minutes' walk away from the stadium. If Matt and Gemma didn't leave in the next five minutes, they wouldn't be able to make it there in time to rescue Matt's family. Also, if they stayed trapped in the basement they would be blown sky-high when the bomb went off!

Beads of cold sweat ran down Matt's face. He leaned close to Gemma. "If you've got another good idea, now would be a great time to share it," he whispered.

Gemma looked miserable. She shook her head.

"Sorry, Matt, I haven't. I think our luck's run out."

Suddenly they heard a growling sound. The bug glowed and in the green light they saw a small dog standing by the door. It had its ears flat against its skull and its lips were pulled back showing its teeth. The bug was much bigger than the dog, but the dog didn't seem afraid.

It darted at the bug and snapped at its legs. Then it dodged back to the door. The furious Insectoid gave chase and the dog dashed out of the room with the bug close behind it. It was the lucky break Matt and Gemma needed.

They raced from the basement and back to the platform. "That little dog was brave to take on that big bug," said Gemma.

"Yes, well, it's not the size of the dog in the fight; it's the size of the fight in the dog," replied Matt. "And that little guy had lots of fight in him."

No sooner had he spoken than the small dog came hurtling along the platform. It jumped up into Gemma's arms and licked her nose. She giggled. "Hey, I think he wants to come with us."

"Why not?" said Matt. "He's saved our necks, so let's save his."

Gemma nodded. "Good call, Matt. Hey, you know what? He's like a lucky charm so we should call him Lucky."

Matt grinned. "That works for me," he said.

At that very moment, a green glow began to light up the platform.

"Quick," said Matt. "The bug's coming. He's after the dog. He doesn't know we're here, so let's go before he sees us."

The Shadow Rangers and the dog scrambled down onto the track and into the tunnel. They made it in the nick of time. The bug skittered onto the platform only to find it empty. It decided it was never going to catch and eat the dog, so it gave up and scuttled back to the basement.

CHAPTER 7

THE BIG BANG

Matt, Gemma and Lucky the dog came out of the Underground station. The street was empty. Lucky sniffed the air.

"Are there any bugs nearby, Lucky?" asked Gemma.

Lucky wagged his tail and licked her hand.

"I guess that means we're safe for the moment," said Matt. "But the Shard is set to blow in five minutes and then all hell is going to break loose."

"Then we'd better run," said Gemma.

"Otherwise we'll never make it to the stadium in time."

Matt glanced around and saw an abandoned, heavy-duty hover transporter.

"Hey, no worries, Gem," he said. "Look at this. It's just what we need."

Gemma wasn't so sure. "I don't know, Matt. It's been here for years. Nobody will have driven it since the Insectoids took London. I bet it won't even start."

"Well, there's only one way to find out." Matt climbed into the cab and pressed the power icon. Nothing happened.

"See, I told you," said Gemma. "Look, we've got less than two minutes before the Shard goes up in flames. So let's go."

Matt rubbed his chin. He knew that the armour-plated hovercraft was just the thing he needed to smash the gates of the stadium so he could rescue his family. He stabbed his finger on the icon really hard. This time there was a whirring sound. The dashboard lit up like a Christmas tree and the craft rose off the ground.

"Jump in, guys," he yelled. "We don't want to be late for the firework party!"

Matt piloted it to a side street next to the stadium and hovered out of sight. Gemma checked the time. "Here we go, Matt," she said. "In five seconds we'll find out if the Insectoids found the bomb or if our plan's going to work."

The two Shadow Rangers felt sick with nerves. They held their breath and stared at the glass-and-steel tower.

Suddenly, bright red flames burst up through it like a volcano erupting. Molten metal and shattered glass spewed out into the air.

Next, a huge explosion shook the ground. The shock waves hit Matt and Gemma's ears like a punch thrown by a heavyweight boxer. The hovercraft rocked and rolled drunkenly. Matt fought to bring it under control. "Hold on tight, guys," he yelled. "This is going to be the mother of all thrill rides."

The red-hot wind picked up the craft and hurled it down the street. They were careering towards the concrete wall of the stadium. Matt wrenched the joystick and hung a carve on the wind like a surfer riding a wave. He gunned the engine and the craft surged back to safety.

"Way to go, Matt," Gemma gasped. "That was a close call."

Then they looked up at where the Shard had been. It wasn't there. It had disappeared in a mushroom cloud of thick, black smoke.

They stared at it open-mouthed, but then broken glass and twisted metal began to fall and batter the hovercraft like a deadly rain. Matt and Gemma flinched and Lucky howled in terror. But the hovercraft's armour plating was up to the job. The debris bounced off its hard shell and they survived the onslaught.

"We've done it, Matt!" whooped Gemma. "We've destroyed the Hive!"

"Yeah, that's great, Gem, but we haven't won till we've rescued everyone."

The Insectoids were already swarming away from the stadium and hurrying to where the Shard had been. They were in too much of a panic to notice the hovercraft.

When the last one had gone, Matt gunned the machine and flew it to the stadium. He smashed through the rusty gates and landed on the centre circle of the pitch. Gemma opened the doors at the back of the vehicle while Matt ran across the grass to his family.

"Come on, guys," he yelled. "I've come to take you home."

His mum, dad and sister stared at him as if they'd never seen him before. Then his dad said, "Matthew, is that really you?"

Matt laughed. He could see his family were in a state of shock. He wasn't surprised after everything they'd been through. "Yeah, it's me," he said. "But we've no time to waste. You can thank me later!"

He ran back to the hovercraft and his family stumbled after him. Suddenly, Lucky started barking like crazy.

"It's all right, boy," said Gemma. "It's only Matt's family."

But Lucky didn't stop barking. He broke free from Gemma's grip and ran at them. His teeth were bared. However, before he reached them a piece of falling debris hit him on the head and knocked him out. Gemma ran over and scooped him up in her arms. Matt was too busy helping his family and other prisoners into the craft to notice.

As soon as they were all on board, Matt hit the
after-burners and the machine roared off. A few
Insectoids who saw them made a feeble effort
to give chase, but they soon gave up. Matt and
Gemma and all the other humans were home free.

CHAPTER 8

A FAMILY REUNION

Gemma was uneasy. "I don't get it," she said. "Why aren't they coming after us?"

Matt pulled a face. "Duh! Their Queen's dead and their Hive's destroyed. They're toast, Gem. So don't worry about it."

Gemma shrugged. "Yeah, I guess you're right."

"You bet I am. Though, to tell you the truth, I'm more worried about what General Carter is going to do to me. He's one mean dude… and I've crossed him."

Gemma grinned at him. "Forget it. He'll have to give you a medal for what you've done. You'll be a hero."

"You think so?" Matt didn't sound so sure.

"I know so," said Gemma. "No Shadow Ranger has ever taken out an Insectoid Hive and its Queen before – even if you did disobey orders to do it."

"Actually, Gem, we did it together so, if I'm going to be given a medal… so are you."

Gemma sighed. She had Lucky lying across her lap. The small dog was still out cold. Gemma stroked his blood-caked head. "Yeah, maybe, but I don't want a medal," she said sadly. "I just want Lucky to get better."

"He will, Gem. We'll give him to the medics as soon as we reach Shadow Ranger HQ. They'll have him fighting fit in no time."

An hour later, they all arrived at the Shadow Rangers' secret HQ. The rescued humans climbed out of the hovercraft. General Carter strode up to them. He had a squad of Rangers with him.

Matt and Gemma stood to attention and saluted. The General stared at them. His piggy little eyes were bright with anger.

"You two are in deep trouble. You've disobeyed orders and I'm busting you from active service. From now on you'll be doing guard duty and nothing else!"

"No, hold up, General," said Matt. "Gemma and I have just destroyed the Insectoids' London Hive and killed their Queen. We've smashed the bugs."

General Carter sneered. "So you say, Ranger, b I've only got the word of two deserters for th

Matt and Gemma were stunned. They knew General Carter was hard-nosed, but they'd never expected him to act like this.

Before they could reply, Lucky woke up. He took one look at Matt's family and began barking like a wild thing.

"Shut that mutt up," snarled General Carter. "Now!"

But Lucky wouldn't stop barking. He wriggled out of Gemma's arms and leaped up at Matt's dad's throat. He ripped the skin away with his sharp teeth.

Matt gasped in horror and grabbed Lucky, but something weird happened. No blood spurted out from his dad's throat. Instead, he pulled at his flesh with his hands and it came away like an insect shedding its cocoon. Matt's mother and sister did the same thing. Only it wasn't Matt's mum and sister… it was two Insectoids!

"What have you done with my family?" screamed Matt. His voice was a mix of fury and despair.

"We sucked out their guts and then used their skins as a disguise." The Insectoid screeched and Matt knew it was laughing. He felt the anger boiling up inside him… but there was nothing he could do.

"Our plan was for you to rescue what you thought was your family and take us to your secret HQ. Then our Insectoid armies would follow us and destroy it – and all the Shadow Rangers."

"Well, that's a shame," said Matt. "Because, thanks to Lucky, we discovered what you were before you could send a message to your Insectoid buddies."

The Insectoids stared at him with their unreadable eyes. "Yes, you have won this battle, Shadow Ranger," said the leader. "So enjoy your victory while you can. I promise you it will not last for long."

"Yeah, right," replied Matt. "Today was the day we got off our knees and kicked your butts. You bugs are history… get used to it!"

"We'll see," sneered the creature. Then it launched itself at Matt. Its front legs came down hard on Matt's shoulders. Matt staggered back. The bug opened its jaws and tried to crush Matt's head. Matt grabbed at the jaws. The bug was strong, but Matt was stronger. Slowly, he forced its jaws apart.

Then Matt's foot slipped and he fell back hard onto the ground. The bug gave a screech of triumph and made to strike a fatal blow. But, before it could, the other two bugs leaped on it and ripped it to pieces.

When they'd finished their grisly work, one of the Insectoids spoke.

"He failed, but we have no wish to die. Spare our lives and we will work for you. You will find us very useful."

"Not a chance," spat Matt. "You bugs killed my family and now you're going down." He pulled out his blaster.

"No!" General Carter yelled.

Matt glanced back at the General. He was pointing a gun at Matt. "Drop your weapon, Ranger… now!"

Matt swallowed hard. He kept his blaster aimed at the bugs.

"We're at war," growled the General. "These traitor bugs are worth more to us alive than dead. So… forget about revenge. We need these two."

"Please, Matt," said Gemma. "Do as he says."

Matt's hand shook. The bugs stared at him. "They murdered my family," he said through gritted teeth.

"They did," agreed Gemma, "but killing them won't bring your family back."

"No, but it'll make me feel a whole lot better."

Gemma shook her head. "Trust me, Matt, it won't… and don't give the General the excuse to shoot you. You've disobeyed him once. He won't back down if you do it again."

"I don't care. They deserve to die."

"Yes, Matt, but you don't." In one swift movement, Gemma stepped up to Matt and knocked the blaster out of his hand. As she did so, a single shot rang out. Gemma gasped as a bullet from the General's gun hit her. She spun round and fell to the ground.

"No!" shouted Matt. "NO!" He sank to his knees next to his friend.

General Carter stood over him. "This is your fault, Ranger. It would never have happened if you'd obeyed orders!"

"Yeah, whatever you say, General," said Matt bitterly. "Look, I don't care what you do to me, but Gemma needs medical help right now and I'm taking her to the hospital."

The General shook his head. "You're going nowhere, Ranger." He still had his gun pointed at Matt.

"Do your worst, General," said Matt. He picked Gemma up in his arms and carried her away towards the hospital.

For a second General Carter watched him with murder in his eyes. Then he lowered his gun and snapped out an order to the Rangers at his side.

"You two go with him and make sure the girl gets the treatment she needs. Then arrest him and put him in the stockade. He can cool his heels in there till I'm good and ready to make his life a living hell."

The two Rangers saluted and ran after Matt.

"What about these two bugs, sir?" asked another Ranger. "What do you want us to do with them?"

"Take them to the interrogation room. They've fallen into my lap and I'm going to squeeze every last drop of information out of them. Then I'll turn them and use them against their bug brothers."

In the background, the two Insectoids glanced at each other and smirked. Although he didn't know it, General Carter had just played right into their murderous mutant hands.

THE END